MIRABELLA'S BEAST

DEANNA YOUNG

For all the wonderful people in the writing community that have inspired me, encouraged me, and helped forge me into the writer I am today, and the one I'm becoming tomorrow. Specifically: Annette Chamberlain, Whitney Hemsath, Heather Warren, Ethan Gramoll, Jayme Phelps, Bambie Childs, Michelle Bulsiewicz, Amanda Mills, Breanna Teramoto, Jocelyn Carlin, Bex May, Karen Hoover, Charity West, Sabrina Watts, Marlene Willis, Kristina Atkins, Julia Allen, Lindsay Hiller, Steve Heumann, Jessica Guernsey, Jenny Rabe, Dyany Munson, Patricia Kornelis, Liesa Hafen, Lugene Ontiveros, Brittany Rainsdon, Yukimi Lumaris, Jennie Bennett, Allison Hong Merrill, Jennifer A. Nielsen, Cherelle Davies, and a plethora of others who undoubtedly belong on this list. If I forgot to mention anyone, rest assured that I've spent a sufficient amount of time laying awake at night wondering how I could have forgotten to mention that very important person by name. I have been fortunate to have so many wonderful people enter my life and guide me through this journey, including those who patiently prod me when I'm not moving fast enough. For that and so much more I will be eternally grateful.

CHAPTER
ONE

Once upon a time, in the not too distant future, the day scientists forewarned and doomsayers predicted, finally came to pass. Whole countries disappeared under rising ocean tides and the seven great continents were reduced to large islands. Humanity survived by constructing massive floating cities, and the world's entire population resided on these gigantic ships. Although this preserved the human race, space and goods were limited. Everyone had to be valuable and contribute to the stability of the species if they wished to partake of the limited resources left on Earth and aboard their ships.

MIRA'S CHEEKS warmed in the late afternoon sun. She stretched, leaning against the faux oak railing behind her. This secluded deck allowed her peace and quiet, along with the ability to watch the bustling crowds several levels below, or stare out over the endless ocean.

Waves splashed against the hull of the ship twenty stories below, stealing Mira's attention for the hundredth time. She closed out of her practice test for the nursing exam and slipped the digi-reader in her pocket. Her brain couldn't handle any more human anatomy quizzes today.

Mira stood and looked out over the edge of the massive man-made island, letting the salty sea air tousle her long, dark curls. It was no grassy cliff overlooking the ocean, like she'd read about in books, but she could pretend, for just a moment.

Shouts from several stories below broke the illusion. Men in an open bay pulled on thick ropes and leaned into their work. She couldn't make out their words, but their voices sounded excited. A net swollen with giant angular fish lifted out of the water. The tuna thrashed in vain against their webbed cage before dropping into an open hold.

Movement caught her eye as rows of solar panels along the hull folded inward, pulling back into storage slots, disappearing from view. The sun still hovered over the horizon, hours from setting. Perhaps a storm was coming?

"Don't lean too far—you might fall in."

Mira turned, locking eyes with Brad, her ex-fiancé. "What are you doing here?"

"I'm sorry, is this deck yours?" He looked around with feigned embarrassment.

She let out an exasperated sigh.

Brad laughed. "I'm kidding. It's good to see you, Mirabella. It's been a while." A deep dimple accompanied his broad, wolfish smile.

"Sorry, I didn't mean to imply you couldn't be up here. I just thought I was alone, and you startled me."

"Of course you're alone." He lowered his voice conspiratorially, "You're not supposed to be up here. But, don't worry, I won't tell."

"The stairs weren't blocked off, so I figured it had been opened up again," she lied, trying to sound innocent.

He winked and pointed up at the administrative towers. "You really should pick less obvious places to hide. I saw you from my father's office."

She looked up at Governor Wilhelm's office window, high above them. "I'm surprised you recognized me from there." She wondered if he really had been up there, or if he'd used other means to find her location. The ship was full of hidden cameras and people willing to spy for extra rations or cushy appointed positions.

"I'd recognize you miles away. You do stand out, you know," he said.

The way his eyes roved over her body, she knew he wasn't referring to the faded orange button up blouse she wore, or the threadbare jeans that had seen better days decades ago, when they'd belonged to her mother. Compared to his crisp collared shirt, sharp slacks with a trendy thin white pinstripe running up the center, and perfect hair that seemed to repel the wind while her own curls whipped around her face, she looked like a frazzled mess. Yet, somehow his tone implied so much more.

Mira's face grew hot, and her stomach twisted tight. Old, familiar feelings threatened to surface. She had to get out of there. "I'm sorry, Brad. I have some place I need to be." She moved around him, heading to the stairs.

"Mirabella, wait." He grabbed her arm. "I've been worried about you lately. Have you thought about how the new protocol might affect you and your father?"

She wrenched her arm out of his grasp. "What new protocol?"

He cleared his throat. "It's for citizens who are unable to work. They will no longer receive government support. If their family cannot help them, they can be transferred to a job they *can* do, or they will be let go, to preserve precious resources."

"Let go?" Mira stared incredulously. That was the term they used when selecting whether a pregnancy could be carried to full term or not. If the baby was not fully healthy or had any kind of abnormality they considered a defect, they were 'let go.' The patient didn't decide, nor did the doctor. The government did. Mira and Brad both should have had older siblings to watch out for them and commiserate with, but that was stolen from them before they were even born. It was one of the things that had drawn her to him, because he was someone who understood. Or so she'd thought.

He shrugged. "Everything possible will be done to find them a job, of course, but too many citizens are mooching off the system, and we have limited resources. Families will simply have to plan for retirement now rather than depend on government retirement. That's all."

"Why now? When was this voted on? How have I not heard of this before? What about the hundreds of citizens expected to retire in the next few years who've been counting on government retirement?" Mira's head reeled with questions. She rubbed the goose bumps forming on her arms. "There's still plenty of room in the city. There are two empty apartments on my block alone."

Brad brushed the hair out of his eyes as a gust of wind blew from behind. "It's about more than space. It's about resources." He pointed to the group of men below, still working on getting the fish into the hold. "That's a really big catch. Guess how long it'll last the city?" He didn't give her a chance to answer before continuing. "Two days. That's it. The schools of fish have been unpredictable lately, catches aren't guaranteed, and we've had months of lower than usual success. And that's not the only problem. Resources are far more limited than most people realize. You don't have to take my word for it. Go ahead and look it up. The order was just made public today. But senior officials voted on it months ago, per the advisement of a city-wide growth assessment committee."

Mira scoffed. "And how many of these committee members will be affected by this order?" She shook her head. "I'm guessing none." This was so typical.

"You needn't worry. Your father has several years left to save, and you live in one of the smallest, most affordable complexes. So long as you have a solid income, you'll be fine. And if for some reason you're not,"---his eyes briefly flitted to her ring-less hand—"I'd be willing to help."

Mira turned, starting to walk away, but Brad stepped in front of her, placing his hands on her shoulders to stop her. "Look, I didn't mean to upset you. Let me take you to dinner. We can talk things over while we catch up."

She shrugged his hands off. "I can't. I really do have plans, and I'm already running late."

Before he could say anything more, she rushed away. The metal stairs clanged with her heavy footfalls, drowning out his attempt to call her back.

She passed a surprised guard when she was nearly on one of the landings. He didn't seem to be expecting anyone to come from above him. "Hey, what's going on? Where are you going?"

She ignored him and kept going, knowing he wouldn't leave his post to chase her unless she posed some sort of serious threat. Lucky for her, she didn't look very threatening.

Once her feet hit the main deck, she raced to the transportation platform, boarded the next tram, and collapsed onto a seat, her shaking legs no longer able to hold her up. Hopefully, the guard didn't see the need to have someone track her down. If he had, she was sure the guard lazily leaning against the door at the back of the tram would've confronted her by now. The city was nothing if not efficient.

Mira rubbed her arm where Brad had grabbed her earlier. How could the committee do this? What were they thinking? And why did Brad have to be the one to tell her? She couldn't help wondering if he enjoyed making her worry. As if that might drive her back into his arms. Her stomach lurched. That wasn't going to happen.

CHAPTER
TWO

AN HOUR HAD PASSED, and Mira still felt shaken. She pulled a tiny cake from the oven and set it on the table where the rest of her father's birthday dinner waited. She'd hoped Brad was making everything up or exaggerating to get a reaction, but her research had confirmed that the proposal—with its manipulative language and supposed scientific predictions—was real. If the governor could get something like this approved, what else was he capable of?

Maybe people would finally start listening to the Free Citizens Committee. They had been trying to depose Governor Wilhelm for over a decade. Then again, maybe people *were* listening. They just weren't doing anything about it. Like her.

Mira's hen, Gloria, clucked from her perch on the balcony.

"Calm down. You'll get the leftovers, I promise."

The chicken tilted her head in jerky motions, as if truly considering that.

Mira laughed and opened the pocket door leading to the balcony to give her some stale bread and fish tails.

Gloria clucked excitedly, pecking at the old food.

While the hen was distracted, Mira pulled a lever on the coop she'd built out of old scraps her father brought home, releasing a single egg into a chute where she could collect it. It never ceased to amaze her that she could feed Gloria garbage and get something as amazing as fresh eggs in return.

Gray clouds darkened the sky, and fat drops of rain plunked onto the balcony slats. A gust of wind rattled the blinds and blew the napkins off the table.

Mira shooed Gloria into the little weatherproof coop and slid the apartment door closed.

She tapped her wrist to activate the device implanted under her skin and check the time. Papa should have been home thirty minutes earlier. She sighed and gathered the scattered napkins, setting them next to the pizza on the table.

Papa's umbrella leaned against the wall, forgotten. He'd be drenched by the time he got home. She tapped her wrist device to contact him.

He didn't answer.

Lately, he'd seemed somewhat disconnected and absent-minded, and she worried he was getting worse. What if he slipped on the wet boardwalk or got lost on the way home?

No. She couldn't think like that. He was just running late.

She sat down and pulled out her digi-reader to study, but every sound from the hallway outside brought her head up.

After five minutes of rereading the same line of text over and over, Mira couldn't stand it any longer. She grabbed her jacket and umbrella and headed out, following her father's daily route.

Before she knew it, she was standing in front of a tram, ready to depart. If she left now, she might be able to get to his work before the next tram left, but she could also pass him if the inbound train left even a single minute earlier than scheduled.

The platform speakers played a recording of an old steam engine whistle, indicating that the tram was about to depart. There was no more time to think. She hopped through the closing doors and took a seat.

Mira peered through the sheets of water blanketing the windows. She examined each tram that passed by, knowing it was futile to try to pick out individuals, even without the rain. Her feet bounced with nervous energy as they passed station after station until finally arriving.

She flew out the door, opening her umbrella. A thick fog had rolled in, reducing visibility to only a few feet.

"Papa? Papa, are you here?" Mira scanned the platform, checking the tram a couple of times to make sure he hadn't boarded it behind her. His blue jacket with red elbow patches would be easily recognizable, even through the fog.

He wasn't there.

Maybe he was just working overtime, and he forgot to tell her? She tapped her wrist device, checking. No new messages. Her heart thumped harder. Something wasn't right.

Guards at the double doors leading to the maintenance offices held up their hand to halt her as she approached. "What's your business, here?"

She eyed the pulse guns over their shoulders and swallowed, wondering if they were set to stun, or worse. "It's my father. He works here, and he never made it home. I wanted to talk to someone in the office and see if they've seen him."

The two men looked at each other, then the one on the left pushed the double doors open for her. "The office is at the end of the hall. Go straight there. This isn't a park for casual strolling."

"Yes, of course. Thank you," she said, in too big of a hurry to think about what he had said, and ran past the doors to the office at the end of the hall.

The young man at reception dropped his feet off the desk when she entered and stowed whatever he'd been fiddling with.

"Really coming down out there, eh?" He eyed her dripping umbrella and the puddle forming underneath. "What can we do you for?"

"I'm looking for my father, Sebastian Ricci. He hasn't come home yet."

The young man tapped a button on his desk, and a holographic display floated above it. With a few taps and slides he pulled up a file. "Ah, yes. He's been assigned to sub-sector twenty three, and it looks like his shift has ended." He looked up at her, smiling as if the problem was solved.

"I know his shift ended, but he hasn't made it home yet."

"Well, you can talk to his supervisor and see if he's seen him. Mr. Griffith should still be down in subsector twenty three. He's always there. Here." He scooped a ball of light from his holographic display and dropped it onto her wrist. "That's a temporary access pass. It'll open the elevator, down the hall to the left."

"Thank you."

"If you can't find him, I'm off in another hour. I can help search," he offered with a kind smile.

"Thanks." She rushed out of the office to the elevator.

It wasn't the smooth, clean type of lift she was used to. When she raised her wrist to the scanner, the doors opened with a clunk. Lights flickered to life as she passed some sort of sensor and stepped inside. There were large push buttons instead of touchscreen displays. Mira took a deep breath, pressed s23, and leaned against the wall as the elevator started its long descent.

After what felt like five minutes, the elevator ground to a halt and the doors slid open into a suffocating dry heat. She stepped out onto the landing, and the variegated metal flooring wobbled beneath her feet. Her hand slapped against the handrail for support as she acclimated to the subtle sway. The suspended catwalk extended out as far as the eye could see, crisscrossed by more platforms and catwalks until it disappeared beneath shadows. Above, massive gears and engines groaned and roared. Pipes ranging in size from a chair leg to the size of a small apartment ran in all directions.

The elevator doors closed behind her, and the rat-a-tat-tat of it returning to the upper levels echoed in her ears. With the light from the elevator gone, the room—if you could call the entire underside of the city a room—disappeared into darkness.

Her eyes adjusted to the soft orange glow from a nearby furnace. Electric lanterns hung farther along the main catwalk in front of her, dimly illuminating their immediate surroundings. She swallowed, watching the shadows. The sooner she found her father and got out of there, the better.

"Hello?" She carefully passed several roaring furnaces. "Is anybody here? Papa? Supervisor Griffith?" A trickle of sweat ran down her back.

How was she supposed to find anyone down here in this immense cavern?

Mira rounded a corner, and the shadow of a man became visible. Her heart jumped, and she reminded herself he was just a normal person, not some monster from one of her books.

His form took shape the closer he came, and so did the confusion on his face.

"Who are you?" he asked in a gruff tone. "What are you doing down here?"

He was wearing a trench coat with the collar turned up, hiding most of his unkempt, bearded face. Why would anyone be wearing a coat in this heat? His eyes narrowed into slits, and she backed up as he stepped closer.

"Hello," she said nervously. "You must be Mr. Griffith."

"I am. What are *you* doing down here?" he repeated.

He wasn't as old as she'd assumed he'd be, probably only a few years older than herself. That seemed pretty young for a supervisor position, but what did she know? She shifted her weight and clasped her hands together to keep from fidgeting. "My father hasn't made it home yet, and I thought that maybe he was still down here, and—"

"And you thought you'd come down to a place *you* don't belong and fetch him?" Mr. Griffith said, crossing his arms.

Mira stood tall and put her hands on her hips, trying to look braver than she felt. "It's raining outside, and he's new to this job, and…and I was worried! I'm allowed to be worried about him."

He grunted. "Well, he's not here. Everyone's gone home.

Have someone call me on the comm next time instead of just wandering around down here. It's not safe."

Mira mimicked him, folding her arms across her chest. "Fine, I'll do that. Sorry to have bothered you." She spun around and strode back to the elevator.

She was almost there when she stopped mid-step. A blue jacket with red elbow patches hung on a hook in a partially open locker near the doors.

Griffith had lied. Her dad was still here.

CHAPTER
THREE

MIRA FOUND the supervisor kneeling near a tank and ran toward him, holding the jacket out. "He's here. Somewhere. This is his jacket."

Mr. Griffith stood, cradling something in his hand. "His shift ended over an hour ago. And I haven't seen anyone since."

"Can I just look?" Mira asked, swallowing as she realized how hard it would be to search for her father on her own, but knowing she had to try. "Just tell me where he was working. I'll go look and then be on my way. Please." She clasped her hands together, bringing them to her chest pleadingly.

He stared at her for a long moment, then let out an exasperated sigh. "Fine. But I can't have you wandering around down by yourself. I'll come with you." He looked down at the bundle he held. "I have to take care of these first."

"Thank you." Her chest felt heavy with anxiety, waiting for him to guide her, but she had no choice.

Whatever was in his hands began to wriggle, and Mira jerked back in surprise. Gooseflesh rose on her arms despite the suffocating heat. "What is that?"

"It's a pair of rat pups." He opened his hands just enough for her to see the squirming creatures.

Rats? On the ship? Her father shouldn't be working around disease-riddled rodents. He could get sick. How many more were there?

Mr. Griffith maneuvered around her, walking with a purposeful gait in the opposite direction.

Mira raced to keep up, wondering how long it'd take to 'take care of them.' She really needed to find her father.

He stopped sooner than she expected and pulled a little wooden box off a water tank.

"What is that?" It didn't look like any cage or trap she'd ever seen.

"I've been keeping the mother rat in here. I found her near one of the furnaces yesterday. I knew she had pups nearby because it was obvious she'd been nursing. I've been on the lookout for them all day." He lowered the pups into the box.

He wasn't going to get rid of them. He was saving them.

She couldn't figure this man out. He got so angry with her for being down here and seemed completely put out when she needed his help searching for his father, yet he went out of his way to rescue rats. It didn't make sense.

Mira leaned in for a closer look, unable to dampen her curiosity. She expected to see something grotesque, but instead saw a worried mother furiously cleaning her babies, and nuzzling them close. Her heart strings tugged watching the reunion. The tiny rodents had a short, fine layer of fur that didn't quite hide their pink skin. Their eyes were still closed, and they crawled over the top of each other making barely audible squeaks.

"Aren't rats bad to have on the ship?" she couldn't help asking.

He snorted. "Rats get a bad rap. These are descendants of genetically engineered rats that were made to detect radiation. Their fur starts to grow in bright orange patches when they come in contact with high radiation for longer than a day, and it grows fairly fast. They were the modern version of a canary in a coal mine. Besides, they rarely damage anything, and they're pretty good at scaring off mice. Those little terrors do cause problems."

The mother rat wrapped her thick tail around the pups protectively as they nursed, continuing to lick them. It was odd how something Mira had been told was a nuisance her whole life could be so surprisingly cute and harmless, and according to this man, helpful. She couldn't help smiling at the thought of this gruff supervisor being some sort of pied piper, rat rescuer. Remembering she was on a rescue mission herself, she cleared her throat. "Can we go look—"

"Shhh." He sat the box back on the tank and tilted his head.

The roar of the furnace a few meters away blocked any noise she might hope to hear, but Mr. Griffith took off down the catwalk. She threw her hands in the air, having no choice but to sprint after him.

After chasing him around several bends in the maze-like underbelly of the ship, she finally heard something. A metallic ping rang out above the machinery noise.

Up ahead, a figure crouched next to the hull of the ship. The figure was pounding on something, over and over.

"Papa?"

Mr. Griffith called out before they reached him. "Stop!"

Her father didn't seem to hear him, so Mira repeated the command: "Papa, stop!"

He kept pounding.

"I said, stop!" Mr. Griffith roared. He wrenched her father away from the hull and let him fall to the catwalk floor.

"Papa!" Mira ran to her father and knelt next to him.

He looked confused as she grabbed his hand. "Mira?"

She helped him sit up. "Are you okay?"

He shook his head, as if coming out of a stupor. "Yes, I'm fine. I think."

Mr. Griffith bent, picking up a wrench, along with several pieces of a broken lever. "What were you doing?" he asked through gritted teeth. The low light cast shadows across his face at odd angles, making him look inhuman. Mira held her breath at his seething anger. What had happened to the gentle rat savior from moments before?

Mira's father stood to face his supervisor, rubbing his neck. "I was performing a valve test, and this one got stuck. It started to leak, and I was hitting it back into place before the pressure burst the pipe."

Sure enough, water was leaking out of a joint nearby and the needle on the pressure gauge above it was climbing into the red.

Mr. Griffith reached over and lifted a different lever, then used the wrench to turn what was left of the first lever, closing it off. "Valve checks are a two-step process. You must turn this lever first, then the other. Check your manual, or ask." The needle dropped as the pressure regulated. "On second thought, I don't have time for people who don't think things through on my crew. Your actions could have sunk the entire ship." He paused, giving Mira an almost regretful look. "Collect your things and leave."

Mira froze, her heart stopping. "He's fired?"

Mr. Griffith held up the pieces of broken lever and the wrench. "Yes."

"Can't you give him a second chance?" she asked. The words from her earlier conversation with Brad rolled through her mind.

Her father grabbed her arm and whispered, "Mirabella…this *was* my second chance."

"Humph. Try fourth." Mr. Griffith turned from them to check the gauges.

"This is just another sign that I'm getting too old for this line of work." Her father glued on a fake smile and headed toward the exit. "It'll be fine. We'll figure it out. Let's go home. I've been looking forward to that special dinner you promised all day."

After he got a few steps away Mira turned to Mr. Griffith and whispered, "Sir, please. My father has only ever worked as a mechanic. This is all he knows."

"I think saying he 'knows' mechanics is a little bit of a laugh right now."

"He was just flustered."

"Well, his flustering cost our crew hundreds of credits and valuable time. We're going to have a hell of a time fixing everything without alerting the safety regulators. The last thing I need is a bunch of city inspectors poking around down here and sticking their noses where they don't belong." He waved his hands over the hull. "Not that they wouldn't have a good reason to. There could have been a serious accident."

Mira noticed for the first time that dozens of pipes had been dented and bent out of place.

He shook his head and tapped the pressure regulator making the needle bounce while mumbling to himself. "Our maintenance budget doesn't account for acts of idiocy."

She winced at his harsh words but mustered the courage to ask again. "Please. You have no idea what he's accomplished in his life. He's brilliant. This *isn't* like him."

"I'm done discussing this. I've got work to do before I can go eat *my* special dinner." He turned away from her and started unscrewing broken pipes at their joints.

"Mira?" Her father called from somewhere farther up the catwalk.

"Coming!" she called back, running to catch up to him. The one good thing about her father not working here would be that neither of them would ever have to deal with that heartless monster of a supervisor again.

"Mira, this looks wonderful. Real cheese too? How did you pull this off with all the extra rationing going on?" Her father tucked a cloth napkin into his collar.

"That's my little secret." She winked as she handed him a

slice of pizza. She put a piece on her plate and forced herself to eat a few bites, despite her lack of appetite.

"You shouldn't have had to come find me." He reached over to pat her hand. "I'm sorry."

"Don't be. They shouldn't have transferred you down there in the first place. It never made sense. Besides, we'll figure it out, like you said. We always do." Mira took one last bite of pizza and moved to open the window, letting in cool night air. "I was thinking; I could get a job."

He shook his head, crumbs falling out of his mouth as he spoke. "You won't have time for school and a job."

"I've been pouring over those books for months. If I'm not ready by now, I never will be. Plus, they gave us two weeks off to study." She talked over her shoulder as she unlatched Gloria's cage, then turned back to stir the mock chocolate syrup warming on the stove.

"I'm sure you'll pass, and at the head of the class, whether you studied more or not. You got all the brains in this family. Even mine. Don't know how I'm functioning without it." He pulled a silly face like he used to when she was a child and he was trying to cheer her up.

It had the opposite effect today, reminding her how much he'd aged in the last few years. He looked worn out, like he was in his mid-seventies, not his early sixties. He should be retiring soon. It was past time for her to step in and help out more. It'd be harder with the new protocol, but they could make it work.

She forced a laugh, the gesture itself making her feel better. "Do the brainless still like cake?"

"I'm not sure. I think we better find out." He stuffed the last of his crust in his mouth to make room on his plate.

Mira smiled, pouring the warmed chocolate over the cake before carrying it to the table.

"You're pulling out all the stops tonight," Papa said.

"Only the best for you. Look, I even found one of these." She produced a thin wax candle, stuck it in the middle of the cake, and lit it. "Go on, make a wish!"

He looked at his daughter, raising one eyebrow. "Are you sure you can handle my wish?"

"Bring it on," she said with a grin.

"Let's see. I already have you, and this decadent cake…"

Gloria squawked from the balcony, staring through the window at them.

He chuckled. "Yes, and you, Gloria."

Mira shook a finger at Gloria, as if reprimanding her for interrupting. "I think she just wanted to remind us to save her a piece of cake."

His eyes grew distant. "Do you remember making *real* chocolate cake with Momma every year?"

"Of course, Papa." She thought back on the last time they'd made a cake together, over seven years ago. Mira had accidentally pulled the beaters out of the mixture before turning them off, and cake batter peppered the room. She still found hidden, dried drops of batter now and then when she was cleaning, like tiny reminders that her mother had been there.

"If I knew it'd come true, I'd wish for one more day with your mother. She'd be so proud of you. I'd give anything for just one more day."

Just one more day. That was something he wished for often, and it wasn't surprising that he said it now. She wanted the same thing.

A pool of yellow candle wax gathered on the cake. Her father shook himself, smiled, and clapped his hands together. "I've got it." He closed his eyes and blew so hard the candle fell over onto the cake, going out with a hiss.

CHAPTER
FOUR

"GOVERNOR WILHELM WILL SEE YOU NOW," a willowy woman said, waving Mira into the office behind two armed guards.

Mira nodded, got up, and headed through the tall office doors.

A plump man with a gray flecked beard and thinning black hair sat behind a large antique-looking desk. He motioned for her to take a seat.

"Hello, Mira. It's been a while." He waved his hands, making a floating display of lights appear above his desk. "I have here your request for a work voucher while in school?"

Mira smoothed the hemline on her navy blue summer dress as she sat down, feeling conspicuous in the informal attire, despite the fact that it was the nicest outfit she owned. She squeezed her hands together in her lap to stop herself from fidgeting. "Yes."

"I think we can make that happen," Wilhelm said.

Mira relaxed. She'd thought getting him to agree to a work voucher at all would be a challenge.

"You should know, I was told your father was here earlier, and he applied for several jobs." Wilhelm rubbed his temples and sighed. "But at his age, it'll be a while before an employer picks up his application. A lot of people have been applying for second, even third jobs. New jobs are going to be hard to come by."

"Because of the new protocol?" She forced herself to sound curious rather than angry.

Wilhelm sat up straighter. "Yes, and I don't like it either. But it's better than letting us get to the point where *everyone* starves. We've got to take care of the problem before it comes to that. Rationing isn't enough anymore."

She couldn't help noting that the top button on his dress shirt was undone to allow room for his swollen neck. He could stand to ration a bit tighter. She bit her tongue. Now was not the time for a fight, so she played along. "That's unfortunate to hear."

"Right, we're doing what we must, though, as everyone should." He clucked his tongue, and scanned the floating icons in front of him. "Now, let's see what we have." He flipped through folders and expanded one. His eyes moved back and forth, reading lines of text that Mira couldn't see.

"I do have two jobs. One is a cleaning job at the port-side elementary school, or we also have a busboy job at the community cafeteria. Both are part-time. Which would you prefer? Perhaps both? I could arrange that." He spun one of the holographic screens to face her.

Mira looked at the displayed hours and wages. "Do you have anything that pays more?" She grimaced inwardly as he looked at her in an exasperated way.

"Let me check." He flipped through more screens. "One other job just opened up, and at twice the pay of the others." He paused, and shook his head. "No, I don't think that will work."

"What is it?"

He cleared his throat. "It's a machinist position on the lower levels—your father's old job. They've specifically emphasized that they need someone who is skilled in this area. I'm sure you don't qualify."

She gave him what she hoped was a look of confidence. "Oh, but I do."

He smiled, in a patronizing way, "Do you, now?"

She smiled back. "Yes. I am fully educated on the inner workings of all the mechanics on this ship."

"Young lady, you will be asked to pass a test before you even meet your supervisor."

A picture of the hulking man in a trench coat with a quick temper came to mind. She swallowed, and sat up straight. "I *can* do it."

He tapped his finger on his lip, thinking.

The door creaked open, and Brad entered. "Sorry to interrupt, Father."

He didn't look sorry as he strolled up to Governor Wilhelm's desk and leaned in close. "The Free Citizen committee has filed an official petition and they wish to meet with you later today." There wasn't a hair out of place on Brad's head, and his crisp outfit looked like it was straight off a mannequin at some upscale boutique. It probably was. He wouldn't be caught dead wearing something salvaged from one of the trash islands. She smoothed her dress again and forced herself to sit up straighter. There was nothing wrong with recycled clothing.

His father shook his head and leaned back in his chair. "It's fine. I've been expecting this. Their petition has no grounds. Best to get the *discussion* out of the way," Wilhelm said, not even attempting to hide his disdain from Mira.

Brad turned to Mira, changing his tone immediately. "Hello, Mirabella. Looking lovely, as usual. Father's not giving you any trouble, is he?"

Her stomach tightened at the familiar attention. "No. We're just wrapping up, actually." She stood to leave. "Go ahead and put me down for that job."

"Not so fast." Wilhelm held up his hand to halt her. "Brad, perhaps you can settle this. You know Mira quite well. Do you recall if she has any experience as a machinist?"

Mira stared at Brad and held her breath.

He studied her for what felt like hours.

"A machinist? No. She's not a machinist that I know of."

Her stomach dropped.

"But," he continued, "she is an amazing mechanic. She can take anything apart and put it back together seamlessly. What's the job?"

"Maintenance work for the under-city," Wilhelm said.

Brad whistled. "A lot of responsibility. Sounds physically taxing as well…"

Somehow this job now depended on getting Brad to agree that she was up to the task. Mira looked him in the eyes, silently pleading.

He nodded and gave her a wink. "Yes. I'm sure she could handle it."

"Alright. I'm trusting the two of you," Wilhelm said, tapping the icons. "Report to this address tomorrow morning to take the test." He flung a set of glowing numbers at her. They hovered for a few seconds before sinking into her wrist. He raised one eyebrow at her, and tapped a few times at his display. "That also has your hiring transcripts, verifying that you were in fact the one I sent. They may have a hard time believing you otherwise."

She held out her hand to shake his, trying not to smile too big, overwhelmed with relief.

"Good luck then," he said, dismissing her without shaking her proffered hand as he went back to studying the images floating above his desk.

She left, and Brad followed her out, closing the door behind him. "Wait, Mirabella."

She turned, "Yes?"

"I kind of stuck my neck out for you in there, and you didn't even say thank you."

She cringed at the accusation, though he didn't seem to be saying it with any malice. "I'm sorry. You're right. I just didn't want it to appear as though you were lying for me, or anything."

Although, she had a feeling Wilhelm was about to give her the work assignment before he came in anyway. "I am grateful. Thank you," she said, with complete sincerity. After all, he could have ruined it for her, and didn't.

"How about repaying me by coming to dinner with me tonight? I really would like to catch up."

Mira looked into his sky blue eyes that contrasted so completely with his wavy black hair. He was just trying to be nice to her, and she kept brushing him off. But the alarm bells in her head were hard to ignore.

"Brad, I'm sorry. I can't. I've got to prepare for this new job. Plus, I'm taking my nursing exam in less than two weeks. I just don't have any extra time."

He nodded. "Okay then, maybe I can help you study?"

She held back a sigh. He wasn't giving in. This was a generous offer. Why was she still pushing him away? It was nice to see him being supportive for once.

"Yeah, okay." She smiled at him, surprised that her palms were sweaty. "I'll have to figure out my schedule first."

Just then, the elevator doors opened and the young man who'd offered to help her look for her father stepped off.

"Oh, hello," he said in an overly familiar way, as if they were old friends.

"Hi," Mira replied, trying to be polite as she moved past him to get on the elevator.

"Did you find your dad?" he asked, holding the door open with his hand to continue the conversation.

"Yes, thank you."

"Oh, good. I was wondering about that. Well, see ya around." He waved and walked away, letting go of the door.

Brad hopped in the elevator with Mira, pushing the button to close the door. As soon as they started to descend, he hit the emergency stop button. "Who was that?"

Mira gaped at him. "What?"

"Who was that? Why did he want to know about your

father?" Brad put a hand on the side of the elevator and leaned over her, making her back take a step back.

Her face heated and she didn't know if she wanted to scream or cry. Who was he to be asking these questions? They weren't engaged anymore, and even if they were, she wasn't his property. She should be able to talk to other men without getting the third degree. "I don't know, actually. He works in the front office at the place where my father was working. I only met him briefly the other day. Why does it matter? It really isn't any of your business. You and I are not together anymore. Or have you forgotten that?" She knew it was rude to throw that at him, but it was frustrating to have all of these emotions surfacing. She didn't need this right now.

He looked chagrined. "You're right. I was out of line. I can't help feeling protective. It seemed like he was bothering you." He pushed the button to start the elevator again, along with the button to take them back up to his father's floor.

"Did it?" Mira studied him. He looked sincere, and once again she second guessed his motives. She had been surprised, which could look like discomfort, possibly.

"Of course. Why else would I say anything?"

Mira shook her head. She was so tired and overwhelmed that it was entirely possible she was misreading everything. "Okay. I'm sorry, too."

The elevator dinged, and the door opened. Brad hopped off and pulled Mira out after him by the hand.

Her cheeks heated as she noticed several people in the lobby watching them. She was sure their elevator do-si-do was quite the spectacle. "I really have to go, Brad. I have things to do."

"I know. I just wanted to be sure we were still on for that study date before you disappeared in the elevator, again."

"Yes, you can help me study, but it's not a date." She almost wished it was. There were things she really missed about him. But there were so many things she didn't.

"Alright, alright. It's not a date." He flashed her a smile that seemed to say he didn't believe a word he was saying. He reached behind her and pushed the elevator call button. "Maybe when things slow down, you can find some time outside of your studies for me?"

He smelled so good. The scent took her back in time, and she almost leaned in to kiss him goodbye. She sighed. "Maybe." He had just helped her, and people could change. Why shouldn't she give him a second chance?

The elevator doors opened again, and Mira hurried to get on before she agreed to anything more.

A young woman with bouncy blond curls and tight jeans flitted off the elevator, then looked between her and Brad. "Excuse me?" she said. "Can either of you tell me where Mr. Wilhelm's office is?"

"Yes, it's the one on the end," Brad said, pointing.

"Thank you," she said in a perky tone, moving past them.

Brad turned to watch her as she left. His eyes roamed up and down her body before settling on her backside. He smiled and raised an eyebrow in approval.

"Really?" Mira asked, stepping onto the elevator, the pain of their break-up coming back in full force. He wasn't hers. Not anymore. He could look at anyone he wanted to, but it was the blatant ogling right in front of her that dripped with disrespect, especially after practically begging her for a second chance.

She sighed. He hadn't changed.

She couldn't start making excuses for him, again.

"Thank you for vouching for me back there. I *am* grateful." She pointed between herself and him. "But, I can't do this again."

"What?" he asked as the doors dinged and began to close.

"Goodbye, Brad."

The doors shut before he could respond. She blinked back tears, hating that she let herself be pulled back into his spell, even for a moment.

Two years ago, he had swept her off her feet. Anything she

could want, he gave her. After a few short months, she was completely smitten. Then, little by little, his attention and doting diminished, and his control tightened. Brad had always treated her well, but expected her to bend to his whims. He dictated what she should wear by buying her new clothes and acting hurt if she wore anything else, especially if it was something he knew was from a salvage shop. The last few months they were together he made a schedule for her that she was expected to follow, under the pretense of trying to keep her more organized. The biggest red flag was the fact that he made all the major decisions in their relationship, including his insistence that she didn't need to go to nursing school, dashing her dreams before they fully took hold. Now, of course, she understood he wasn't trying to take care of her—it was just one more way to keep her in his debt. Ironically, it wasn't until she noticed how he treated other women like objects that she realized he treated her the same way. He flirted with other women openly, even when she was around, reminding her often that he could have any woman on the ship, and she should feel 'lucky' to be with him. This was what had eventually broken the spell. He may have loved her, but he didn't value her. She was more than a pretty accessory for him to don when it was convenient.

Breaking off their engagement was one of the hardest things she'd ever done, but this all confirmed that it had been the right thing to do.

Mira shook herself. There wasn't time for this. She pulled out her digi-reader and typed: *city-ship mechanics and schematics.*

CHAPTER
FIVE

MIRA TOOK a seat in the maintenance office after being handed her test. She couldn't help glancing at the door. It wasn't too late to leave and apply for a different job. Her feet bounced as though they were ready to leave the second she gave the okay.

A count-down timer lit up in the corner of the screen. She couldn't run away from this. Her dad was counting on her. She took a deep breath and scrolled up to begin. The questions started out very basic, increasing in difficulty with each one. By the thirtieth question she was solving hypotheticals rather than fill-in-the-blank on parts and general maintenance.

With the clock down to its last three minutes, she reached a question that made her pause. *What would you do if you came upon a release valve lever that was stuck, and needed to be shut off immediately due to building pressure?* Mira bit her lip and tapped in her answer. She hit 'enter,' readying herself for the next set of questions, but none came.

Five seconds later, an alarm sounded. Time was up. She returned to the counter and pinched the display of light that was her test, causing it to collapse into a weightless bar, and dropped it onto the proffered scanner.

It all came down to this. Had she studied enough? Her chest tightened.

The man read the results, lines of unreadable words reflecting in his eyes. He looked up at her, shaking his head.

Her heart seized.

"Well, I guess you're qualified. As far as I can tell, you got a perfect score."

"Seriously?" Mira said, letting out her breath. She resisted the urge to hug the little man. "So, what now? Just head down and find the supervisor?" Her relief was replaced by trepidation as she realized she'd have to face Griffith again.

"Yes. You'll be working with Jim today." He tapped a few buttons, scooped up some light and dropped it onto her wrist. "That's your elevator access. Jim should be waiting for you on subsector twenty-three."

"Got it. Thanks," Mira said, thanking whatever bit of luck had gotten her out of working with Mr. Griffith.

She left the office and got onto the elevator at the same time as another woman, though she was a lot taller than Mira herself and looked like she lifted weights for a living. Mira patted her chest to try to get her accelerated pulse under control. It was one thing to pass the test, and quite another to perform the job.

"Where're you headed?" the woman asked, in an almost accusing tone.

"Subsector twenty-three." Trying to ease the woman's suspicions, she added, "I just started today."

The woman scrutinized her and raised an eyebrow. "Griffith's new hand, huh? You're a bit smaller than I expected. But I suppose I've seen stranger things. He sure likes his misfits."

Mira wasn't sure what to say to that, and luckily she didn't have to say anything. The elevator slowed to a stop at subsector ten, and the woman got off. "Good luck," she said, walking away.

The doors closed and before she knew it, she'd arrived and

was once again standing in the dark underbelly of the city, holding onto the handrail as the catwalk swayed.

"Now what?" she mumbled, regaining her feet and focusing on the walkway directly in front of her. A burst of steam escaped from a nearby valve making her jump, and her heart hammered, thinking of the last time she was here.

"Hello?"

"Hello," came a not-too-distant reply.

She squinted and saw someone coming down the walkway.

As he got closer she could see he was a thin middle aged man, likely in his late forties, with dark skin and a thick, bushy mustache. "I hope you haven't been waiting long, I—" He stopped speaking as he reached her and blinked in surprise. "Sorry, you're, uh, smaller than I expected."

"You're the second person to say that." She straightened her back. "And I'm not that small."

He pulled on his thick mustache, looking her over. "Well, this isn't easy work down here. You've got to have a bit of muscle and grit." He shook his head. "But, we've been shorthanded for days and my wife would love to see me home at a decent hour. So, I'm willing to give you a chance. Don't mess it up, hear?"

"Yes, sir," Mira said quickly.

He led her down a long corridor, passing row after row of intersecting walkways and platforms.

"How come there aren't any horizontal transporters down here? It'd make getting places a lot faster," Mira said.

Jim glanced over his shoulder at her. "Are you tired, then?"

"No. It just seems like a waste of time. We've been walking for almost ten minutes now."

"There are a few transport systems on other levels, but the lower half of this level is periodically flooded to cool the engines for cleaning, check for leaks, put out fires, and test the emergency pump systems. Most of the equipment on this level is manually operated and maintained. That's why we're here."

"Wait. Water reaches up this high? We're still a couple stories above the bottom of the city. That's a lot of water. Couldn't that sink the ship?"

Jim stopped walking and turned around. "It doesn't reach this high, and partitions are raised, so only a small section at a time is submerged."

"Oh."

He squinted at her. "Who hired you? I thought you were a mechanic."

She cleared her throat. "I am…kind of."

He rolled his eyes and threw up his hands. "We asked for someone with experience."

"Well, I'm studying to be one." It was sort of true. She had been studying to pass herself off as one. "And I passed that test of yours. I'm a fast learner too. Just give me that chance you promised." She stood tall, trying to stare him down.

"Fine. We're almost there anyway," he said, turning to continue on, mumbling under his breath as if having a double-sided conversation just loud enough for her to hear. "This one is really too old and a bit forgetful. What should we do with him? *Oh, no problem, send him to Jim.* This one is unstable. Probably shouldn't be working with people. *Just send him to Jim.* This one isn't really a mechanic but wants to be. Where should we send 'em? *I know! Jim.*"

Jim stopped.

In front of them loomed a wall covered in pipes, valves, levers, cranks and geared apparatuses. "Alright, this is where we're working today. Do a good job and you can come back tomorrow. If not…you won't. I'll have to shadow you today, to make sure you know what you're doing."

Mira swallowed as a dry lump settled in her throat.

"Okay, our main job today is to check pipes for leaks. Record the leaks, if there are any, and fix them. Got it?" Jim said, talking slowly as if Mira wouldn't be able to follow along.

"Got it. Do we bleed the lines or just open and shut off each valve? Do we also check the main gates, or do those remain closed at all times unless we're using them?"

He raised a brow, appraising her. "We *do* need to bleed the secondary lines, but not the main lines. And yes, the gates will need to be opened and resealed. It's the best way to check for gaskets that are wearing down. We'll do the gates first. And afterward, maybe we'll go our separate ways so that we can get done faster—if it looks like you can handle it."

Mira nodded, feeling more confident. "Got it."

To Jim's surprise as well as her own, she performed task after task seamlessly that day. Before too long, he was letting her do things on her own and only came to check on her occasionally.

Finally, he approached her and patted her on the back. "You did good today. Meet me at the elevators tomorrow. Nine a.m. sharp."

"Yes, sir," she said and made her way out of the subsectors with a little more spring in her step than when she entered.

CHAPTER
SIX

OVER THE NEXT FEW DAYS, Jim and Mira worked several sections of the sub-levels together. She was getting in the groove of this juggling act between work and school. She rarely saw anyone other than Jim during the day. Mr. Griffith showed up to talk with Jim once in a while, sometimes looming over Mira while she worked, but he never stayed long. Thankfully.

"Ready to open this puppy up?" Jim said as he walked over to a large furnace door.

"Sure." She got up from the pile of dried seaweed bricks she'd been sitting on.

He stepped up to the furnace and grabbed one side of a giant wheel. "Once we open her up, we have to clean her out and check for corrosion." He pulled on the wheel in quick hand over hand motions. It popped open, singing a high note as it swung out.

"Climb on in," Jim said, his voice echoing inside the cavernous chamber.

Inside, a slick gray film covered every surface, thicker in some areas than others. After an hour of scrubbing, Mira's arms felt like lead weights had been tied to them, and her shoulders were threatening to go on strike, but she pushed on.

Eventually, Jim threw his rag onto the growing pile by the door. "Nicely done. Easy enough, right? Just two more to go."

Mira groaned, not sure if her joints could handle scrubbing two more furnaces. But she didn't complain aloud, afraid to show she couldn't handle this job.

Luckily, the other furnaces were much smaller, and they spent most of their time repairing worn vents.

"Alright, on to the last job for today. We'll be checking valves, just like the first day. Think you can do it without me breathing down your neck?" Jim asked.

Mira stretched her tight shoulder muscles and smiled. "Yeah, I can handle that."

"Alright, just go that way, until you reach sector E." Then he pointed in the opposite direction. "I'll go this way, with the more complex valves. When we're all done, we'll meet back here. Record any unusual readings on the pressure gauges as you go. If any of them are in the red-zone, contact me immediately." He tapped his wrist a couple of times and held it over hers until it flashed. "Just tap it three times, and it should connect you directly to me."

"Got it."

"Oh, I almost forgot"—he held up a finger—"you're heading into a hot-zone. If a pipe is painted red, do *not* touch it without gloves. If you forget that, you'll really wish you hadn't. Here." He handed her a pair of old leather gloves, then turned and left.

The work went quickly, and after what felt like only minutes Mira realized she had traversed nearly two hundred yards down the sector. A line hissed as she released steam from a valve and hot water dribbled onto the floor. No leaks so far, no worn gaskets or problems. With how often these were checked, it wasn't surprising.

The rhythm of the nearby engine hummed like a lullaby, and she had to fight to keep her eyes open. Working and studying so much was catching up to her. She hoped she could make it through her internship while working this job—if she passed the exam next week. She blinked and stretched, releasing a yawn, glad the day was almost over.

From the corner of her eye she thought she saw movement, and the metal flooring several yards away creaked. She turned to get a better look, but saw nothing other than hundreds of yards of open catwalk and pipes.

"Hello? Jim, is that you?" There was no reply. Her tired brain was making her paranoid. The only sounds were that of water flowing through pipes, engines turning, and the unnerving subtle groaning of the metal hull moving through the water.

She rolled her eyes at her childishly-active imagination, and continued toward sector E. She was nearly done.

A few minutes later she reached the end of the sector and started to turn back, but saw one solitary light halfway down the catwalk in sector E. Strange.

"You done?" a voice asked through her wrist device, startling her.

She tapped it and responded, "Yep. Just got done. I'm going to go turn off a lantern that's been left on at the end of sector E, then head back."

"No. Leave it. Your job is done for the day. Let's go home."

"You sure? It'll only take a minute."

"Yeah, come on back. We're done."

Mira shrugged. "Okay, boss." She jogged back to the junction where Jim was waiting.

"Any problems?"

"Nope. Everything looks good."

"Great. Let's go home." His mustache twisted up into a smile. "You're doing good here, kid."

Mira beamed at the compliment, ignoring the 'kid' part. "Thanks."

As they made their way to the elevator she reached for her digi-reader to study as they walked.

It was gone.

"Jim?"

"Yeah?"

"I dropped my digi-reader. I've gotta go back for it."

"We can get it tomorrow. I'm not paying you to get your digi-whats-it."

Her stomach twisted at the thought of leaving it behind. "I really need it tonight. I've got a big test that I'm studying for. Just clock me out when you get up top. You can do that, right? I'll be right behind you. I swear."

Jim tapped his wrist, noting the time, and sighed. "Okay. I'll clock you out. Just hurry. This sector is supposed to be cleared in an hour for submersion. They like everyone to be out of the lower levels at least half an hour prior, so they'll be shutting down the elevators about then."

"Don't worry. It's not going to take me that long," she said, running in the opposite direction, scanning the catwalk as she went.

By the time she made it to the end of sector F, she was losing hope that she'd actually find the digi-reader, wondering if it'd dropped down to the lower levels or got left behind in one of the furnaces.

Turning to head back she saw it peeking out from behind a pipe, near the wall.

"Oh, thank goodness," she breathed, scooping it up and clipping it securely to her belt.

Looking over, she noticed the lone yellow glow in sector E again. Jim hadn't wanted her to bother with it before because he was eager to get home, but she had no reason not to go turn it off now. It'd take less than a minute.

Upon reaching the light, she stopped mid-motion before she flicked it off.

A curtain hung over the doorway of a make-shift room only a few meters ahead. It had been hidden by pipes before.

Curiosity pushed her forward over a narrow plank that straddled the gap between the catwalk and the strange room. She lifted the curtain, revealing a large chamber.

Along the back wall were rows and rows of books. Actual, real books. Her heart fluttered, and she read the titles on the spines. From what she could tell, there were medical books, fairy tales, romance novels, children's books, historical fiction, encyclopedias, and even an atlas or two. Why were they down here of all places? She resisted the urge to scoop up an armful and take them home with her.

Furniture took up the majority of the moderately-sized room. Someone was living here.

A potted bush rested in the middle of a small table. Roses? They weren't the typical color she associated with the plant from pictures she'd seen. The blossoms were vibrant yellow, transitioning into orange with deep red at the tips. Like a sunset captured in a flower. Where did this come from?

She stepped into the room to get a closer look, bending down to touch one of the silky petals. As she did so, a single yellowed leaf fell, dropping onto the table.

"What are you doing here?" someone roared, shattering the silence.

Mira clapped her hands over her ears and turned to see Mr. Griffith entering the room.

CHAPTER
SEVEN

MR. GRIFFITH PUSHED her out of the way, as he yelled, "What do you think you are doing here? Get out. Get out now!"

Mira stumbled backwards, too stunned to offer an apology or an excuse.

"Out!" he roared again.

She scrambled to the door, skirting around him, yanking the curtain so hard it fell in a heap behind her as she darted through the gap.

It felt like her feet weren't even touching the metal as she ran. Her lungs burned. She chanced a look over her shoulder and thought she saw him following her but couldn't be sure.

She forced herself to keep running.

Tears filled her eyes, and she wanted to scream in frustration. How could she be so stupid? Even if she passed the nursing test on Friday, she'd need a good paying job to get her through the internship phase. She'd be fired for sure after this.

Just as Mira rounded the corner to meet up with the main catwalk, a horn blared. She shrieked, lost her footing, and tumbled to the floor rolling with too much momentum on the shaky walkway. She groped for something to stop her and grabbed a pipe.

A red pipe.

Searing pain shot through her hand and she lurched away.

That final movement propelled her body under the railing and off the side of the catwalk.

She screamed and groped for something to stop her, slapping her hand on a support beam beneath the ledge. The pain from the fresh burn poured down her body in a wave, and she released the beam before she could stop herself.

Her heart jumped into her throat and every muscle tightened as she dropped.

She collided with a group of wires, stealing the air from her lungs. It slowed her fall long enough for her to grope for a handhold. She remembered to use her good hand, but the wires snapped, and flung her face first into a pipe.

The hollow gong of the impact echoed around her and she fought through the pain and fuzz to stay conscious.

She twisted around just in time to land flat on her back on top of a pile of wooden crates. It snatched her breath away and her stiff body tumbled down the wooden mountain, landing hard on the floor of the city-ship, while boxes toppled and crashed around her.

Too stunned to move, she lay still, taking in what had just happened. There wasn't a single part of her body that didn't hurt. Warm blood tickled her skin, rolling from her nose toward her ear. She brushed the hair out of her face and wiped her nose, cringing as she touched it. When did she hit her face? She couldn't even remember.

Her nurse's training kicked in, and she tried to calm herself so that she could assess her injuries while lying there.

Her entire palm was badly burned, along with the bottom half of all of her fingers. She shook as she examined it more closely. Some of the skin was peeling away to reveal shiny pinkness underneath. Swollen blisters took up the other spaces. The burns were likely only superficial, despite how much they hurt. Next, she touched her ribs gingerly, definitely bruised, but not broken. There was a large knot on the back of her head and, of course, her broken nose made it hard to breathe.

She could still move her arms and head—but not her legs.

Something was terribly wrong.

She sat up, noticing for the first time that her legs were pinned under a large crate. Why couldn't she feel them?

"Well, this is just great."

Distantly, Mira thought she could hear water. Like someone had turned on the sink in a bathroom far away.

Her eyes went wide, and her hammering heart somehow beat even faster.

They'd begun immersing the sector.

"No. No. No. No." She pushed on the crate with her good hand.

"Help!" she screamed. "Somebody help me!"

She tapped frantically at her wrist device. "Jim!"

No response.

She pulled up her contact list, selecting every single person. "Help me! I'm stuck on the bottom of the ship and it's about to be covered in water. I can't get out." She looked around for some sort of reference. "When I fell, I was leaving sector F, only a hundred meters or so from the elevator. Please hurry," she said, trying to keep the panic out of her voice.

A thin rivulet of icy water coursed across the floor. Mira gasped as it wrapped around her. She pulled desperately at her legs, hoping the crate would float when the water level rose higher. But it didn't.

She snatched a slat from one of the broken crates and used it as a lever to lift the other crate. It started to lift, then with a crack, the wooden slat snapped.

The cold water climbed up past her navel. Her breath caught and her body trembled. It couldn't end like this.

"Help! Somebody, please! Help!" she screamed, knowing it was futile.

As the water reached chest level, she remembered Mr. Griffith. He was down here. He could save her.

"Mr Griffith! Help! Please, I'm trapped! Please!"

What seemed like mere seconds later the water level was at her shoulders, and she couldn't hold it together any longer. Huge, hot tears rolled down her face.

She lifted her arm out of the water, checking her device. No one had responded yet. Not even her father. She tapped the line, "I love you, for always, Papa," and ended the simple message as the water licked her neck.

Her chin trembled, and she screwed up her face, fighting against the overwhelming panic to let out a final, throat-numbing scream.

The seawater crept up to her jaw, and she tipped her head back, sucking in deep breaths until her mouth went under the rising tide.

Within seconds her entire body was submerged.

Adrenaline rushed through her, and she yanked at her legs again.

The giant object shifted.

Yes!

She tugged harder, pushing against the heavy crate with both hands. With each push she grit her teeth against the instinct to gasp, blowing out to release huge air bubbles instead. The effort drained her, but she couldn't stop trying. She gave one final push with everything she had left, and it shifted again, but not far enough before settling back down.

It wasn't working.

She couldn't die like this.

She couldn't leave her father alone.

This couldn't be the end.

Her lungs demanded air. The pain in the rest of her body was all but forgotten. She had to breathe in to relieve the burning but knew she couldn't.

She fought to keep her mouth closed, but it opened against her will. She gulped the frigid water in like she was taking a deep breath. Her lungs spasmed and sucked in more water. Every muscle in her body seized and her vision closed in.

CHAPTER
EIGHT

MIRA CAME TO, dragging in a halting breath.

Someone stood above her talking, but she couldn't comprehend the words.

Her stomach muscles tensed, and she turned onto her side, heaving. The vomit burned like lava as it came out through her mouth and nose. Pain returned full force. Everything hurt.

For what seemed like several minutes, she lay there, gasping and coughing before the spasms died down, replaced by uncontrollable shivers.

"You're going to be okay," a deep, gentle voice assured her.

She looked up to see a shirtless man kneeling over her. Water dripped off his hair and beard, running down over his chest. Slits fanned out on his neck. Were those gills?

She blinked. Her eyes were playing tricks on her. Maybe she was dreaming? No, the pain was too real.

"Mr. Griffith?" she asked in a slightly nasal voice. "You saved me?"

"Looks like it," he said, relief evident on his face as he reached around and gently lifted her to a sitting position. "What happened?"

She cleared her throat and coughed a few more times,

wincing at the feeling of broken glass rattling in her lungs. "Well, I got a little freaked out by *someone*, and managed to slip and fall while running away." She wiped a drop of blood from her nose and gasped at the rush of pain.

"Careful, it looks like you broke your nose." He leaned in closer to look at her hand. "What happened there?"

"Red pipe." She pointed to the offending piece of metal behind him. "I grabbed it just before I fell." She felt uncomfortable beneath the gaze of his somehow familiar gray-blue eyes and dropped her gaze, staring at the slits on his neck again, instead.

She opened her mouth to ask if they were gills when he seemed to notice her stare.

He turned away from her and put his trench coat back on. "We need to get you someplace more comfortable until the elevators come back online." His guard came up, along with his collar, and the gruffness she'd seen during their first encounter returned. "It'll be awhile. Can you walk?"

"I think so." She grabbed a rail with her good hand and pulled herself up. A wave of dizziness hit her and she leaned into the railing for support. "Maybe give me a minute," she said, sitting back down.

He shook his head. "I don't know why I asked. You're in no condition." He slid his arms beneath her and lifted her up, supporting her against his chest.

Her pulse slowed, and she relaxed, settling against him. "Mr. Griffith?"

"Damon."

She tilted her head to look at him.

"My first name. It's Damon."

She swallowed. "Damon, I'm sorry I invaded your privacy earlier. I didn't think—"

"No," he interrupted. "I'm sorry. I planned on apologizing to *you* tomorrow. I'm used to being left alone. I didn't expect anyone to be there. I overreacted. Seems to be a flaw of mine."

"No, I really am sorry—"

"Stop. I've behaved terribly around you. I could make a dozen excuses, but none of them would be good enough. Your apology makes mine feel hollow, as if it's unnecessary. I should have never behaved that way."

She wasn't sure what to say. He had behaved horribly, but none of it was without cause. She thought about how curiosity had driven her to invade his privacy when she went to shut off that light. "We all have our flaws."

"Right. You came down here to find your father, I acted like a crazy person, and you actually came back here to take his place."

"I had to. I needed this job."

"Exactly. You did what you had to do, even when you didn't want to. I'm not half that brave. Plus, Jim has nothing but praise for you."

She laughed uncomfortably. "Oh, I have plenty of flaws. You just don't know me well enough."

He adjusted his grip to hold her more securely. "Well then, challenge accepted. I'll just have to get to know you better."

Although he probably meant nothing by it, she became keenly aware of his body heat penetrating her wet clothes and his hand on her thigh.

She squirmed a bit so that he loosened his grip and tried to change the subject. "So, Damon, I've never seen a rose in real life. That is what it's called, isn't it?"

He nodded. "They were a gift from my mother; the last thing I got from her before she died. They're meant to look like the sunrise, to remind me of the mornings we spent together when I was small. But they haven't been doing very well lately. I guess I'm a bit protective." There was pain in his voice as he spoke.

"For what it's worth, I'd be a bit protective of them, too."

He grunted some sort of assent and for several minutes, neither of them spoke.

A groan followed by a high-pitched whine echoed across the expanse of the ship.

Mira jumped and pulled herself closer to Damon.

He laughed. "Don't worry. It's just the pumps kicking on." He pointed up ahead with his chin. "And we're here."

He carried her inside the little apartment and set her next to the couch. "You'll need to get out of your wet clothes."

She shrunk, scanning the one large room. There were no separate chambers for privacy.

He rummaged through a dresser and brought out an old uniform. "These coveralls will be huge on you, but it's better than nothing."

She felt heat rising through her. Definitely better than nothing.

Heavy exhaustion settled over her and she grabbed the back of the faded brown couch for support, then jumped, suppressing a yelp as pain shot through her hand, lost her balance, and stumbled sideways.

Damon caught her arm and steadied her before she fell over. "Woah. Are you going to be okay if I step out while you change?"

"Yeah, I'll be fine. I just lost my balance. I wasn't passing out or anything. I promise." She gave him an embarrassed smile.

"Alright." He looked skeptical, but he nodded at the doorway behind him. "I'll be right outside if you need anything. Just holler when you're done." He grabbed a shirt out of the dresser, then he turned and disappeared behind the curtain.

Changing was difficult. She was only able to use one hand to remove the wet clothes clinging to her body, and every movement made her more aware of her bruises and scrapes. Her tight shoulders didn't want to bend as she hooked them into the sleeves. But she got them through, zipped the ugly thing up, and sat on the couch, relieved.

"I'm done," she called out, sniffling back blood that had started to drip from her nose again.

Damon returned and put a kettle of water on the stove, then

grabbed the blanket from the small twin bed and arranged it across her lap.

She pulled up the contact list on her wrist device, while Damon rummaged through a cabinet on the other side of the room. She recalled and deleted all the messages she'd sent out, none of which had been read. A rock sunk in her stomach knowing that no one would have come to her rescue if Damon hadn't been there, but it did no good to dwell on that. So she shook it off and tapped out a new message to her father explaining where she was, letting him know she'd contact him in the morning. He had likely gone to bed over thirty minutes ago anyway, and she didn't think she could handle the emotional toll it'd take to go into everything that'd happened right now.

Damon seemed to be on auto-pilot as he came back over with a beat-up first aid kit, took her hand, and smeared burn cream on it.

She stifled a scream as the cream brought the pain in her hand to life again, stinging and growing hot, before finally cooling and blissfully numbing everything it touched.

Damon wrapped it gently with gauze, then applied bandages to the other visible cuts and scrapes on her face and arms. Her heart skipped around erratically and she wasn't sure if it was from her injuries and the lingering anxiety from her near-death experience, or Damon's unexpected attentiveness.

She felt like a damsel in distress being ensnared by the charms of her rescuer, and it annoyed her. She wadded up a piece of gauze and gingerly pushed it into her nose. He was being kind, and she was grateful. Nothing more.

"Thanks," she said, with a more pronounced nasally voice, running her fingers over the bandages with her good hand. "You did a really good job. If I didn't know better I'd think you were in nursing school too," she said, cocking an eyebrow.

"Nope. All my schooling comes from those books." He thumbed over his shoulder at the shelf overflowing with books of all shapes and sizes. There had to be hundreds there. Most were paperbacks with worn and faded titles on their spines, but quite a few had solid hard covers with aged and flaking metallic lettering.

"How *did* you get all of these?"

"Guilt payments from my father, mostly." He pinched his lips together and gave a slight shake of his head, as though he hadn't meant to reveal that part. "But some were gifts from my mother. She was a school teacher, and an avid reader. I've always loved reading. There's not much else to do when you're stuck down here."

Mira nodded, then hissed, bringing her hand to her head as pain exploded behind her eyes. She wanted to say more about the books and share her own love of reading with him, but the throbbing in her skull made it too hard to form thoughts into sentences.

Damon's brows knit in concern. "I don't have access to pain medicine, I'm sorry." He moved to the stove, poured a steamy cup of tea from the kettle, and brought it back to her. "But I've got this. It should help."

She sipped the steamy brew and sank back into the couch, savoring the warmth spreading through her body. Despite trying to stay alert, she started to drift off to sleep. She vaguely felt the teacup being removed from her hand and her body being lowered onto the couch before the sweet bliss of dreamland swallowed her whole.

———

Hours later, Mira woke to a pungent smell and a soft tapping sound. She was disoriented as her eyes struggled to focus. Moving to sit up, she forced her stiff legs to obey her commands.

"Ow!" Her entire body screamed in protest.

Damon looked up from the stove, where he was stirring something. "Good morning. Ready for breakfast?"

She wrinkled her nose, surprised that the smell could penetrate the gauze she had stuffed up there. "Sure."

He plopped lumpy yellow mush onto a plate and brought it to her.

It seemed to be some sort of egg substitute. Hopefully, it tasted better than it smelled. Definitely not what she was used to, but it'd feel good to get something in her stomach.

He got a plate of his own and sat down across from her. "Sleep well?"

"Yeah, I think so." She rubbed her stiff neck.

"I was worried when you conked out last night. I thought maybe you'd passed out. But once you started snoring, I knew you were fine."

"I don't snore," she said, through a mouth full of eggs.

"Well, if you don't snore, the language you talk in your sleep is awfully guttural."

She gaped at him and pointed to her face. "It's because of my nose…and this cotton. I don't normally snore." She removed the rolled up gauze, careful not to pull too hard and make it bleed again.

"Uh, huh." He raised his brows. "I think I found your flaw."

She laughed, and grabbed her ribs. "Ouch!" She tossed a pillow at him. "Don't make me laugh. It hurts."

He batted it to the ground with a chuckle. "How bad is it? Need more tea?"

"No." She put her hands up to ward off the question, along with the tea that had knocked her out the night before. "I'm sore, and it hurts if I move too fast, but other than that, better than I expected."

He looked her over and nodded. "You're one tough biscuit. Sorry, I don't have any real pain medication."

"I'm fine. Really. What was in that tea, anyway?"

"It's my own concoction of herbs. The devil's claw in it helps with swelling, and the willow bark is an aspirin substitute. The devil's claw is pretty bitter, so I add mint leaves for flavor."

What must it be like to live down here, away from everyone else, without access to the little things she took for granted? "But why don't you have access to regular medicine?" she asked before she could stop herself.

He ruffled his hair, and it gave him the appearance of a madman. "Well, you don't think it's normal for someone to be living down here, do you?"

She almost laughed as she took in his manic appearance, but she bit her lip and shook her head.

He shrugged. "According to the ship system, I don't exist. If you don't exist, you can't buy certain goods."

"How does that work? You have a job. You're a supervisor, for goodness sake."

He looked away. "I'm an anomaly. I was never supposed to be born. I was never implanted with a fancy tracking device in my wrist, because, according to doctor's records, I died at birth." He moved his hands to the collar of his coat, hesitated, then took it off, revealing the slits again. "I was my mother's first child. They knew by the second trimester that something was different. You're a nursing student, so maybe you've heard of pharyngeal arches?"

"It sounds familiar, but I don't remember what they are," she said.

Damon grabbed a tattered book from the floor by the couch and flipped to a well-worn page. "Well, fetuses go through a stage in early development where it looks like they have gills, right?"

She nodded, leaning forward to see the sketch on the page.

"Those are the arches," he said, closing the book. "Mine actually did develop into gills, and they told my mother that she needed to *stop me from maturing* and *let me go*. But she refused. Her husband loved her enough to agree to hide me. I lived with them, and my little brother—officially their only child—in secret until I was ten. That's when mother died, and father moved me down here. I guess he didn't *let me go* out of love for her, but he didn't like the risk of having me around either. I got books and rations for years, then, one day all of that stopped." He shrugged. "What happened after that is a bit hard to explain because I had a rough go of it for a while, but the short version is simple. I took a job down here, and was able to get a ration card activated, which is where my pay is deposited. Then I worked my way up to supervisor just like anyone else would."

"Wow," Mira said, pulling the blanket up under her chin. She wanted to ask more about his life down here but found herself asking instead, "How was your mother able to stop them from taking you all those years ago?" Tears stung the corner of her eyes, and she blinked them away. "My mother was forced to abort my older sister because she would've been born with chromosomal abnormalities."

He looked down at his hands. "I'm sorry. That should've been my fate, too. My father used his government connections to stop it, I'm sure."

"Who's your father?" she asked, trying to recall any officials with the last name Griffith.

"Nobody," he said, "I'd rather not talk about *him*."

Noting his tone, her eyes moved to the roses, then to the plate now devoid of egg substitute. She had fresh eggs at home, thanks to her mother. It was a luxury that most in their station could only dream of. "I have a chicken," she said.

"What?" He looked at her as if she'd grown a third eye.

Mira laughed. "I mean, I have something special from my mother, too, like your roses. It's a chicken. Mother saved for years to buy Gloria. She brought her home only a few months before she passed away."

"Why a chicken?"

"She grew up on a farming barge, outside the city. She became orphaned as a young teen and survived by rummaging through the trash to find scraps for her pet chickens, then eating the eggs. I guess she got Gloria to remind me of who she was, and where she came from. She was tougher than I'll ever be."

"I doubt that," Damon said, gathering the dishes off the table and walking them back over to the sink.

"I worry about what it will do to Papa when that chicken dies. He's already lost two daughters—my older sister Sabrina died when she was eight, and the one that was *let go*. Then, my mom died two years ago. They had me when they were a lot older, I never even knew Sabrina. Anyway, I'm all he has left. He's all I have too."

"He's lucky to have you, Mira," Damon said.

His sincere smile and intense eyes sent a thrill though her, and she had to look away. "Thanks. I'm the lucky one, though. He's always supported me, through everything."

Suddenly, her eyes popped open wide. "Oh. I was supposed to contact Papa this morning. He's probably worried sick after my message last night." She tapped on her wrist, and saw several missed calls from her father. Of course he'd been trying to reach her. She hit the 'return call icon,' but there was no answer. She tried again, and again it went to voicemail. It made no sense. Her heart started to pound as worry and dread filled her chest. She scrolled over to her inbox displaying her messages. There was a new message there. But it wasn't from her father. It was from the North-Point Hospital.

CHAPTER
NINE

MIRA TAPPED THE FLASHING MESSAGE. *"Sebastian Ricci has been admitted to North-Point General for multiple injuries requiring surgery. You may present this letter at the front desk to gain admittance to his room. Regards-Dr Levitt."*

She gasped, covering her face with her free hand. Her insides turned into a tornado and she couldn't think clearly with her mind spinning so fast. What had happened to him?

"What's wrong?" Damon asked, trying to crane his neck to see the message.

"My father's in the hospital. I have to leave." She tapped out a quick letter to her father, letting him know she was on her way, and turned the haptics on her wrist device to their max, so she wouldn't miss his call again.

"When will the elevators be back up?" Mira asked.

He stood and looked out the door. "Shouldn't be too long. Maybe thirty minutes? It's mostly drained."

Mira raised herself up, grimacing as her muscles objected to the motion. "I need to go."

Damon moved in front of the door. "You can't just leave."

She started, taking in his size for the first time since her rescue. "But, my father needs me." She scanned the room for other escape options.

"Of course," he laughed. "I mean you can't leave by yourself. You're in no condition. Plus, you probably want to get back into your old clothes." He popped up the collar of his trench coat again, running his fingers through his hair, flattening it down. "They're over there." He pointed to the clothesline next to the stove where they were hanging. "I'll wait outside."

"You're going with me to the hospital?" she asked.

He frowned, and a cloud fell over his features. "No. But I can ride up to the main level with you. We'll find someone to escort you the rest of the way there."

"Oh," she said, realizing she'd really rather it was him. She could use someone to lean on right now, and not just physically.

He seemed to notice her dejection. "I'm an anomaly, remember? It's too risky for me to go with you, especially to a hospital."

She nodded, understanding.

As soon as he was out of sight, she painstakingly changed clothes again and met him outside. "Alright, let's go then."

Before long they were turning the corner toward the elevators. Mira stared at the spot where she'd rolled off. The water was low enough she could see the wreckage below. She shivered, rubbing the gooseflesh that popped up on her arms.

Damon put out his arms, blocking her from getting too close to the railing and guiding her around the corner, skirting the slats where she'd thrown up.

As they approached the elevator, she sat against the wall, next to the locker where she'd first spotted her father's jacket. It seemed like ages ago she had wandered down here searching for him. Her heart ached that she couldn't keep him safe, despite her best efforts, and her mind raced through multiple scenarios of what could have happened to land him in the hospital.

The red light above the door blinked, indicating it was still offline.

"You can go back. I'm sure I can make it from here," she said.

Damon sat down next to her. "I'll stay. I said I'd take you up to the main level, didn't I?"

"True. And I kinda like your company." She smiled, resting her hands on top of her bent knees.

"Mira?"

"Yes?"

"Thanks for—for not being freaked out about my condition." He pointed to his neck to clarify.

"Well, I snore," she said, shrugging.

He laughed. "That's true."

She bit her lip, wondering if she should say more, and rushed on before she lost her nerve. "I don't think anyone would freak out over you being an anomaly. I mean, you're obviously very capable, and resourceful, and the things that make you different, also make you better. It's like the rats. Everyone has been taught that they're bad, and they blindly believe it. I did. It's easy to demonize something you never actually see. But seeing you with them opened my eyes. People need to see you, too. They need to see how wrong we've been. How wrong all our policies are." She was being such a hypocrite right now, and she knew it. It was unfair to even suggest he should do more. After all, she'd never once gone to one of the Free Citizens meetings, and she'd never stood in protest against the Governor. But someone needed to, or things would never change.

"Mira, I can't. You might accept me, but others won't. Trust me on this." He reached over and patted her hand, squeezing it gently before letting go.

Her stomach fluttered. His touch was so reassuring. Then again, if her time with Brad had taught her anything, it was that she was prone to seeing what she wanted to see in a guy and ignoring everything else. She was probably misreading Damon right now, seeing things that weren't there simply because she wanted them to be. He was just a guy being nice to a girl who had been clumsy enough to nearly get herself killed.

. . .

Still, she was surprised at how comfortably familiar it felt to be near him now. She leaned back farther and tilted her head toward his. Not quite touching him, but enjoying his proximity.

"So, why nursing?" he asked after a few minutes of silence, shifting to get more comfortable.

"It's a stepping stone. I couldn't afford to go directly into med school. One day I'll be able to get my doctorate and be part of a research team for Porter-Alan's disease or Alzheimer's."

"That's ambitious. I sense a story behind those specific diseases."

Mira nodded. "My mother died of Porter-Alan's, and Alzheimer's runs on my father's side." She cleared her throat unsure if it was still raw from the trauma yesterday or if she was getting choked up thinking about her father. "I'm beginning to see the first signs of it in him…it scares me. I—"

A loud buzzing noise interrupted her, and she looked up to see the light change from red to green.

"Oh! It's online again, right?" Mira used Damon's shoulder to push herself into a standing position.

"Yep. Let's go."

Within minutes they were both in the break room relating their tale to Jim.

"Well, you look terrible," Jim said.

"Uh, thanks," Mira touched her face self-consciously.

"If you wanted to get out of the desalination cleaning, you could have called in with the flu, or scurvy, or something. You didn't need to go through all that." He shook his head in mock disapproval.

"I'll keep that in mind for next time." She wondered for the first time if she might have to pay for all the damage she'd caused, and her stomach twisted. They couldn't afford any more surprise expenses.

"So, you need an escort to the hospital?" He stood and straightened out his pants. "I've got an hour before I have to clock in. This paperwork can wait."

She started to say she'd be fine, but the look on Damon's face stopped her.

He ran his fingers along the upturned collar of his coat. "Maybe it would be better if I took you. It's been raining this week. It's normal to be wearing something like this."

Jim raised his eyebrows and shook his head. "I hear that they have someone who's agreed to sign up under that new protocol thingy. He'll be the first. The Governor is going to be at the hospital today to witness the signing. That hospital will be crawling with guards and reporters."

Mira felt sick. Why did this new protocol feel like a personal attack? She thought it was supposed to be a few months before it went into effect too. She turned to look at Damon, hoping he could read her expression. She wanted him to come, but he couldn't. It was too risky.

He shook his head slightly, seeming to understand her silent plea. "Jim, make sure someone at the hospital looks her over. She's been through a lot more than she's letting on."

———

Mira and Jim could've walked to the hospital, but they decided to take the tram, hoping to get there as soon as possible. Their shortcut turned into a long delay when the tram broke down on an overpass. They weren't allowed to disembark and instead had to wait helplessly until the repair was completed.

What should have taken them less than ten minutes took them over an hour, by the time they finally arrived.

A TV in the hospital lobby played propaganda commercials about the citizens' duty to sacrifice for the greater good, obviously leading into the main event to be held there later. Mira cringed at the blatant brain washing.

After checking in, she made her way through the halls with Jim on her tail, finally reaching the wing with her father's room.

Two armed military officers flanked the door. Their crisp

uniforms made them look more official than the ones she saw stationed throughout the city.

She looked at Jim and pointed behind the officers. "It was this room, right?"

He scratched his head. "Yeah, that's the one."

Mira stepped between the officers and put her hand out to grab the handle.

The taller officer pushed her back. "You can't go in there."

"That's my father's room. I was sent a summons by the hospital." She tapped on her wrist device, pulling up the message, and turning so that the officers could see the image. Her ears grew hot, and she tried to ignore the anxiety building inside.

The officers exchanged a look, and the smaller of the two waved her forward. "Alright, you can go in." He pointed a finger at Jim. "But you have to stay out here."

Jim put up his hands, warding off trouble. "Sure, sure." He looked to Mira. "You good? I should probably get back, anyway. My shift started almost ten minutes ago." He tapped his nose and pointed to hers. "Have someone check out your injuries while you're here too."

"Thanks, I will." She waved to him and pushed the door open.

Her father was sitting up in bed, reading some papers on a clipboard. A nurse fussed with some tubing dangling from an IV bag on the other side. Three other people were in the back of the room, setting up camera equipment.

"—now this is just ceremonial, of course. We'll have all the official stuff written up later," said the man who had been holding the clipboard seconds before.

It was Governor Wilhelm.

The room seemed to expand and all the voices sounded miles away.

Mira felt light headed.

She stumbled to her father's bed, steadying herself against the wall. "Papa? What's going on?"

"Mira!" he said, the relief evident in his voice as he reached out to pull her closer to him. "I've been trying to reach you." He pushed her back to look her over. "Are you okay? What happened to your hand?"

"I'm fine, just a little work accident. Are *you* okay?"

He shifted in his bed, and looked down at his hands. "I went out for a walk yesterday afternoon and fell. I broke my shoulder and bruised up my hip pretty good."

She slid the clipboard off his lap and held it out of his reach while she read the words in bold black ink. There were blank signature lines at the bottom. "What is this?" her voice was barely audible. She was drowning all over again. Air refused to enter her lungs.

"History in the making. That's what," the Governor said. "Your father has agreed to be the first to sign."

"What?" She looked at her father, hoping he'd deny it. The pained expression on his face told her it was true. This couldn't be happening.

Without pausing to consider her state at all, Wilhelm pointed to the papers in her hand. "A provision in the new protocol allows those with terminal diseases the option to terminate early, in exchange for a lump-sum payment to be transferred to their family."

"I thought the whole idea behind this was to save resources. How does paying people make sense?" Mira said, somehow speaking through the fog in her head.

A man came up behind Wilhelm, excited to point out a colorful poster with graphs leaning against the wall, apparently made for some sort of presentation. "It does save resources. It saves on medication that would have been administered. In most cases, that medication hardly helps anyhow, wasting it. It'd also save on housing, hospital care, hospice, and food costs. We've done the math. A lump sum payment is by far the lesser of the costs, but leaves the individual a way to contribute to their family before they leave. It's best for everybody."

"No! No, it's not best for everybody," Mira said, unable to keep the anger out of her voice. "I guarantee that none of you will be subjected to this 'voluntary termination.' You won't ever be in the position to need to choose. This is murder! How can you not see that?" Hot tears spilled from her eyes as she spoke.

She yanked the papers from the clipboard and tore them up, letting the pieces fall to the floor. "He's not signing!"

"Mirabella," her father pleaded.

She could see the resignation in his eyes. The peace. "No, Papa. You can't." She dropped to the floor beside him and leaned her head on the bed next to his. Sobs tore from her chest. "Please, no," she sputtered.

"Sweet, Mirabella. Listen to me. I'm already dying. During the surgery they found a tumor. It's inoperable. And my liver's failing. I have a year at the most, but it's likely I have less than six months. If I do this, I can leave knowing your schooling has been taken care of. You wouldn't be left with mountains of debt. I want to do what is best for you, while I still can."

Mira stood and turned away.

Unable to contain the frantic energy inside of her, she kicked an empty chair, sending it skittering a few feet. "This isn't what's best for me!" she screamed. She crossed her arms across her chest to keep from falling apart and stood at the end of his bed. "Listen. I don't care if I have to work overtime for the rest of my life. It would all be worth it knowing I had a little more time with you, even if it was just one more day." She returned to his side and held his hands, blinking back tears. "Just one more day," she repeated.

Her father dropped his head, looking at her hands in his. "I want to do something for you before I'm gone. I don't want to be a burden."

"You're not a burden. You're family. I need you."

Governor Wilhelm cleared his throat, interrupting them.

"He's already agreed to the deal. Unless you can come up with a way to pay off these hospital expenses, with this new diagnosis he will automatically be put in the societal burden category, as it is." He waved someone over, and they handed him a new set of papers. He calmly secured them into the clipboard and set it back on the bed. Her attempt to stop him hadn't even slowed him down. "This is a way he can leave on his own terms, and help you before he goes."

Every head turned as the door to the room slammed open dramatically.

"Mirabella?"

"Brad?" Mira said.

He looked her over, taking in her swollen nose and disheveled appearance. "What in the world happened?"

"Just a work accident. I'm fine," she said, looking away. Why did he have to be here?

Brad strode to Mira, taking her hand. "I heard what was going on. I saw your father's name on the news and came to see if you were okay."

She couldn't look at him.

He let go of her hand and addressed his father. "I will take on this family's burden, as my own."

"I can't let you do that. The burden will be too great. You have a future family to worry about." There was something about Wilhelm's speech and mannerisms that seemed rehearsed.

"This could be my future family," Brad said and turned back to Mira. "If you'll marry me."

Puzzle pieces fell into place and realization hit. Was he actually using this new protocol to trap her?

She pulled her hand out of his and looked down at her father.

She'd have to agree. What other choice did she have?

"Just a second," she said, standing and walking to the back of the room, forcing herself to breathe and think.

"Well?" Brad prodded.

"I don't have to go to nursing school. There's no reason to

incur that debt right now. I can work extra shifts until I pay off the hospital bills."

Wilhelm scoffed. "Look at yourself. You're hardly in any shape to work extra shifts. And from the looks of you, I'm sure we'll need to do a thorough safety sweep of all the subsectors. The inspectors might come back to say that it's unsafe for you to work there." She understood the implied threat. Play along, or we'll make sure you pay for more than the debt alone. She thought about Damon and what might happen to him if they did do a *thorough safety sweep.*

Mira faced Brad, every muscle in her body tensed. She looked at her father, lying in bed, with the clipboard back on his lap, concern etched on his face.

"Okay. I'll do it."

Brad smiled victoriously.

"Stop!" The door banged open for the second time.

Mira did a double take, looking back and forth between the man in the doorway and the man standing by her father.

Two Brads?

No.

His eyes were gray-blue, not sky-blue, and his shoulders were more broad. Their features were almost identical, but their style was not. Brad wouldn't be caught dead in a trench coat.

"Damon?" she asked, shocked. He had shaved his beard and his hair was cut short, but it was him. How had she not seen it before?

He looked at her with wide-eyes. She couldn't tell if it was fear, shock, or some other emotion.

"Damon?" Brad said in astonishment.

"What are you doing here?" the Governor demanded.

"You can't do this," Damon said. "Enough is enough." His hands curled into fists and he took several steps toward Wilhelm.

Mira moved forward and gently pulled on Damon's arm, stopping him from getting any closer to his father. Once he seemed relaxed, she let go. The last thing he needed was an assault charge leveled against him. Especially with no witnesses to what had really happened.

She backed up a few steps to give him some space and bumped into the camera, poised and ready to record.

"Hey, watch it!" Someone on the camera crew said.

Witnesses.

The camera.

She coughed into her hand and Damon turned to look at her. She raised her eyebrows, hoping he'd understand why she got his attention, and subtly glanced at the camera. Confusion crossed his face for a split second, then he stood a bit taller and dipped his chin in agreement.

"Sorry about that. Let me fix it." She grabbed the camera and repositioned it, ignoring the annoyed looks from the camera crew. Before she let go, she pushed the red 'record' button and turned back to face Wilhelm.

This was her chance to stand up against all the injustices. It didn't matter if she lost her job, if she was buried in mountains of debt, or was banned from ever attending nursing school, she had to do this. She addressed Wilhelm but spoke loud and clear for the camera. "This man saved my life yesterday. You should be proud of him, not hiding him away."

Wilhlem snorted. "You don't even know what you're talking about. If you did, you wouldn't be so quick to defend him."

Damon shook his head and removed his trench coat. The slits on his neck stood out against his pale skin.

"What—what is that? How did you…who are you?" the man with the charts stammered.

Damon grabbed Brad's arm and pulled him to his side. "Who? Can't you tell? I'm Damon Griffith Wilhelm, eldest son of Governor Wilhelm, the hypocrite."

A collective gasp rebounded through the room, and the man with the charts looked like he might faint.

Wilhelm pointed a finger at Damon. "You are not supposed

to come up here! You are breaking your part of the deal. I've protected you all these years, and this is how you repay me? By trying to disgrace me?"

"Protected me? You mean you scared me. You told me that people would be afraid of me; that they'd shun me, and try to kill me. But no one I've ever met has treated me as poorly as you."

"You are a disgrace. A monstrosity. A freak. You never fit in, and you never will. Go back where you belong, before I'm forced to let the law find you, like it should have years ago."

Mira could hardly believe what she was hearing. How could a man say those kinds of things to his own son? "Yes, he is an anomaly, but without this difference"—she reached up and brushed her hands near his gills—"I would've drowned. No one else could have rescued me. Please, listen. Our differences make us better, not worse."

The chart man harrumphed, apparently recovering from his earlier shock. "We are simply trying to save humanity by conserving resources and—"

"Trying to save humanity?" Damon said, interrupting him. "Which part of humanity? Why do you get to decide who deserves to live? What about the anomalies?"

The man arched his back, standing defiantly against the questions. "Most anomalies wouldn't live past a few months, and the rest would have such a low quality of life it would be cruel to force them to bear that burden."

Damon scoffed. "No. Cruel is telling people that your ideal is all that matters. Cruel is teaching people to be afraid of someone who is different."

Mira raised her voice, pleading with the Governor. "Don't you see? We are stronger because we all have different strengths, not because we can all fit into the same mold. We should be encouraging variety within our species." She took her father's hand and smiled at him. "We should be embracing our older generations, learning from them and sharing in the kind of wisdom that can only come with age. That is what will ensure our survival. What we look like doesn't matter. It's what we *do* that makes us what we are. The only monstrosity I see in this room is you."

Governor Wilhelm wagged a plump finger at her. "I do what needs to be done—what others don't have the stomach for. My job isn't always pretty, but someone has to do it."

"Why are you the one that gets to decide what has to be done?" Mira said, glancing at the camera, reassured to see it was still recording. "You are supposed to be protecting us. Yet, you and your supporters want to cull our population. You want us to ration, tighter and tighter." Her face was flushed with color and she swallowed back the congestion caused by the tears she was trying so hard not to release. "How can you expect this of us, when you don't even follow the rules yourself?"

Wilhelm lunged at Mira, faster than a man his size should have been able to, and Damon stepped in front of her, blocking him.

The impact of running into Damon's immovable mass knocked Wilhelm unceremoniously to the floor. "Your little speech isn't going to fix the problem," Wilhelm grunted, rolling to a sitting position. "We've still got resource problems that are only going to get worse."

"No, you're right." Her mind raced, knowing she needed to say something or she'd lose this debate, and the stakes were too high. A thought formed in her mind and she ran with it. "Well, we could start by not making chickens so expensive. That's never made sense to me. They are natural recyclers, taking our scraps and turning them into food. Every household should have several, not just the elite."

The chart man spoke up. "Not a bad suggestion, but it won't solve everything. It's a mere drop in the bucket."

"Maybe that's just it. The solution is more than one answer. We can fill that bucket—one drop at a time. We have a ship full of smart people who are capable of thinking of ways to solve these problems that don't involve euthanasia."

Wilhelm laughed. "Smart? Yes, the ship is full of people smart enough to do what they are told and not get in my way. They are smart enough to know that one signature from me can render any of them a 'burden to society' and you'd do well to remember—" Wilhelm cut off abruptly and his eyes bulged.

Mira followed his line of sight to the blinking red light on the camera.

"Turn that thing off!" Wilhelm bellowed, crawling like a madman toward it.

Brad seemed to wake from his stunned stupor and quickly crossed the distance, shutting it off.

Loud voices in the hall caught Mira's attention. Some sort of argument with the guards ensued, and seconds later a mob of people poured through the door.

A middle-aged-woman pushed her way to the front of the crowd. "Mr. Wilhelm, as president of the Free Citizens Committee, we can't let you sign anyone to this new protocol. You've gone too far. No more slaughter in the name of preservation. Your time as governor is over."

Wilhelm hauled himself off the floor with enormous effort. "You have no power here," he said, panting.

"Actually, we do. We've got piles of paperwork explaining why. You love paperwork, right? You've always loved throwing laws in our face. We'll let you read all about it on our way to the courthouse where you will peacefully resign. We're not waiting another day," the woman said.

"I want all your names," he said, adjusting his suit over his plump body. "Brad, call my lawyers. Have them meet me at the courthouse. This isn't over."

Someone in the group grabbed his arm, and he jerked it away. "Don't touch me. I'm coming peacefully."

The crowd filed out and the camera crew followed, leaving Mira, her father, Damon and Brad alone in the room.

"I've got some phone calls to make," Brad said, turning to leave.

When he reached the door, Mira called out, "Brad…"

He paused, with his hand resting on the handle.

"I'm sorry." And she was sorry for the position he was in, but nothing else.

Brad didn't answer. He simply leveled a glare at Damon and stormed through the door, slamming it behind him.

Damon melted into the chair by the bed. "I can't believe I did that."

Mira rested her hand on his shoulder. "I'm just glad I wasn't misunderstanding your signals back there." She laughed, feeling an ache in her shoulders as she finally relaxed. "Are you going to be okay?"

He grabbed her good hand and pulled her down to sit on the arm of the chair. "I should have done it long ago. I just never had enough courage. Maybe you're rubbing off on me," he said with a half-cocked grin.

She smiled back. It was such a shock when he burst into the room. He looked so different with short hair and a clean shaven face. It'd take a while to get used to that. "By the way, how did you know I was here?"

Damon leaned back in the chair and took a deep breath. "When I went back down to the sublevels I couldn't stop thinking about what you said, about people needing to do something if they wanted to see things change. Then, I saw the news, and recognized your father's name. I knew my father was behind all of it, and I knew this was my best chance at confronting him. I chopped off my hair and gave myself a shave, knowing it'd be more believable if he couldn't deny my relation to him. After that, it's all kind of a blur."

"And the guards just let you in?"

"Looking so much like my brother had the added benefit of confusing them, I guess."

"Wow." She shook her head. "I don't know what else to say. These last few days have been absolutely crazy."

"Ahem." Her father cleared his throat.

"I didn't forget about you, Papa," she said, moving over to the bed and hugging him as tight as she dared.

"You know, not to brag, but my birthday wish may be coming true," her father said.

"And what was that?" Mira asked.

"I wished for you to find more friends. People you could turn to when I'm gone. I won't be here forever, and being alone is a beastly burden." He waggled his eyebrows at her. "And, maybe you've found more than a friend, eh?"

"Papa!" Mira said, shocked. "I barely know Damon."

"Ouch," Damon said, clutching at his chest. "You save a girl twice and she says she barely knows you."

"I mean, not yet…I mean, I don't know what to say about that." She poked her father. "Don't do that!"

Her father laughed, looking at Damon. "Thank you. I owe you everything."

"Anyone would have done the same thing, Mr. Ricci."

"Not anyone. You risked a lot coming up here."

Damon shrugged, then cleared his throat. "Speaking of owing, I owe you an apology for—"

Mira's father cut him off. "Don't. You were obviously right. I shouldn't have been down there. Ten years ago, or even five years ago, I could've rebuilt half the ship blindfolded, but age has obviously caught up to me." He gestured at his bed and sighed. "I was too stubborn to see it, and too worried about Mira's future to simply give up."

Damon shifted in his seat. "Still, I'm sorry. I should have handled it better. I was worried about the ship, of course, but I was also worried about being discovered if anyone came to investigate what had happened. I honestly didn't think people would accept me if they knew what I was." A genuine smile lit his face and inclined his head toward Mira. "But I was wrong. She did, without a second thought."

"Leave it to my Mirabella to see the beauty in others and then help others to see it too. You know that is what her name means, right? To see beauty."

"Fitting." Damon nodded, then stood. "I suppose I should be getting back to work."

Mira fiddled with the bandaging on her hand, gathering her courage yet again. After everything she'd just done, this shouldn't have been so hard. Damon reached the door and she cleared her throat. "I have that nursing exam coming up soon. Think you'd be up for helping me study?"

"Of course."

"Good." She took a deep breath. "Then it's a date."

He grinned. "It's a date."

———

A few days later, Mira tiptoed through her apartment, readying herself for the day as quietly as possible. She didn't want to wake her father. He needed his sleep.

Her nerves were surprisingly calm, considering that today was the day of the big test. After all that had happened over the last few days, the nursing test seemed pretty insignificant, but her dream hadn't changed.

She slipped on her jacket and opened the door, then paused.

There on the doormat was a single rose the color of the rising sun resting on a card.

She opened the card and read, *You've got this. Go change the world. -Damon.*

Mira grinned, pressing the card and flower to her chest. Her world had already changed forever.

ABOUT THE AUTHOR

Deanna Young grew up in northwest New Mexico doing all the normal things a child of the desert does. She chased lizards and climbed cottonwood trees, built 'inventions' out of junkyard scraps, and grudgingly dealt with the ever-present New Mexican sand that seemed to take up permanent residence inside her shoes. It was amongst this gritty environment that Deanna discovered the value of stories. Whether spinning yarns for her siblings during the years they went without access to TV, or sitting on her father's lap while he read The Hobbit over and over until the cover wore thin, she learned that stories are about more than mere entertainment. Stories are about immersion, inspiration, and connection with others, both inside the pages and out. Love of the written word stayed with Deanna when she traded the majestic New Mexican mesas for the humble Oquirrh Mountains in northern Utah, where she currently resides with her family. Although she often misses the starry skies, dramatic sunsets, and mouth-watering green chili of her youth, she doesn't miss the omnipresent sand and heavy shoes. As a mother and/or caretaker to four kids, nine chickens, two cats, and a rambunctious dog she has plenty to keep her occupied. Thankfully, she still finds time to coax new creations out of her imagination and onto the page. Deanna's work can be found in several anthologies, including: Once Upon a Future Time Volume I and Volume II, A Fantasy Christmas—Tales From the Hearth, Something Lost, and Something Found. Deanna has also received accolades for her works including first place for the opening chapter of her nonfiction memoir Half Blue (yet to be published), and the Grand Prize for her flash fiction story The Scarf, which can be read at: https://www.saltandsagebooks.com/posts/2019/flash-fiction-grand-prize-winner/Flash Fiction GRAND PRIZE WINNER - Salt and Sage Books

Deanna's passion for storytelling, along with her writing skills continue to evolve and grow as she draws inspiration from her own life and the world around her. Follow her on Amazon, Facebook, and Instagram.

www.ingramcontent.com/pod-product-compliance
Lightning Source LLC
Chambersburg PA
CBHW032022180726
48283CB00008B/2798